Hello,
Allen,

we ... people heard you are coming to stay. You can come any day, and you never have to go away. So let your trip begin as we have a special for you at our Inn. Best always.

Michael McCann

Welcome
Travelers please sign in

_____
(write your name here)

On this planet when the children run through the fields, their toes tingle, their smiles jingle, and the animals mingle.

Cats and dogs all get along
and always exchange hats
as they talk with the bats.

At night when the children finally sleep and do not wiggle, all the parents get together and giggle.

It is a place where time can stand still and some times it will. When people come and stay it is hard for them to go away. Everyone can hardly wait for another day.

Thus begins the story of a purple place that some says looks like a pumpkin, but you must ask that story from a local bumpkin. Come travel with us to a special place, where people have a special grace and the sky is as soft as purple lace.

Remember when you are ready to travel to Purpleumpkin, you can not go by car, you will not get very far. You can not go by plane, you will not make much of a gain. You can not reach the top of the bow by train. Noo, Nooo.

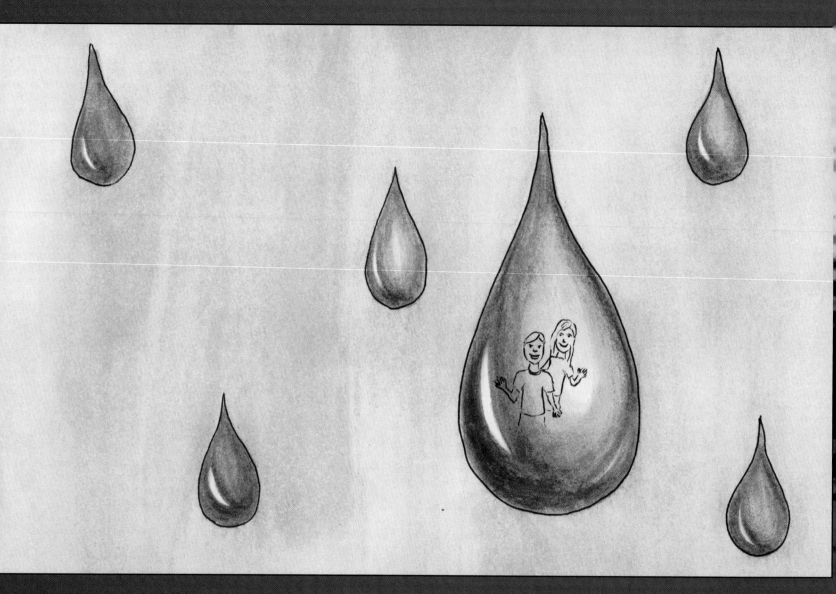

You can only travel in a drop of rain.

To make much of a gain to start this relation, you must all gather to leave from a rain station. When you get to the rain station to start your trip and relation, you will meet a man who will help you hop into the rain drop.

He is the man of the sky and we know why. He makes sure the rain is clean and clear for generations so dear. He makes sure the water is so pure, he can give it to us and his friends the otters for sure. His name is Al and is Earth's and Purpleumkin's special pal.

When you leave the station to travel up the rainbow with all your friends and family in tow, as you near, all faces will be a glow with a smile as there is only a mile to go. Then you will finally get to know the magic place with a special grace, and the sky of purple lace.

When you arrive at the magical purple place, you will be met with friends with a special grace. They are the makers of purple here, they are known as Murples so dear. You will find they really care. They love all people, animals, and living things, who come. No matter what country or world they are from.

That even includes your sister and brother, your father and mother, your grandpa and grandma, and all the friends you will meet along the way, as you learn more every day. The Murples hope we will learn to think and try to be this way. It makes for such a beautiful day.

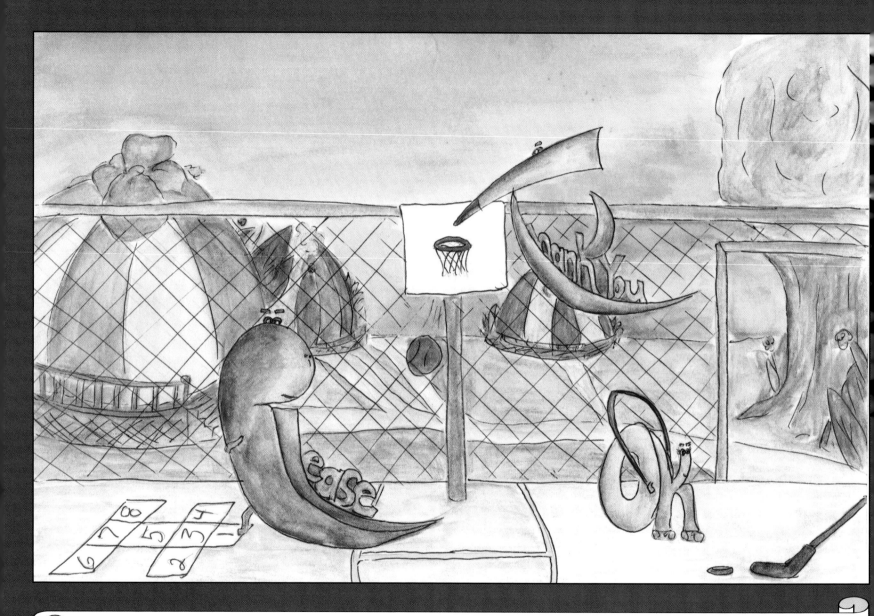

After you meet and spend time with the Murples, they will introduce you to friends who also like you and Purples. Their names are Please and Thankyou. They are special at fun and games. One never goes far without the other.

When you ask to go out to play on a certain day, you will say Please right away. On that day you will get to meet Okay. If you say Thankyou, then Thankyou will follow and go with all of you when you go on your way, even on another day.

Later in the day Please, Okay and Thankyou will introduce you to more friends as you travel on your way. They are Dick and Joanne. They are keepers of the land. They are very kind and grand. If you have a problem they will help you understand.

When crossing the street they will make it safe to meet. You always, always look both ways. Before you go, they will teach you to hold hands, and make it safe to go on your way, here and at home for another day.

As Dick and Joanne teach you more rules of the land, they will take you to a special stand. They will introduce you to Patti, who wears a special Hattie. She will meet with, greet you, and she will eat with you.

It is important that you have a treat, and to eat, so you will be strong as you walk down the street. She will make you feel good and well to have something to eat so swell. Patti is such a great cook, you will not just be able to look. She will make you something so special, you will be able to read this book.

After a good lunch, Patti will introduce you to a special bunch. Their names are Bailey and Lori, and they want to teach you a special story. When you visit their home, you will see it is shaped like a dome. It has a large flower on top that has an aroma so sweet and pure. A home fit for Murples and friends for sure.

As you walk around you will see they have no windows or doors, just floors. How could that be? You will smile with glee and Lori will let you see. When Lori wants to go in, she will use her finger like a pen, and draw the windows and doors in. At the end of the day when everyone is through, she simply will wash them away and draw them in on another day.

Bailey and Lori have a special way which they celebrate everyday. It is about music and being neat, which they will show you without missing a beat. They will teach you how to put your toys away everyday while singing and playing a song along the way.

You can sing or play a song and they will all join along, and quickly they will be gone, in a special way for another day.

As it gets later in the day, Bailey and Lori will bring you along the way. They will introduce you to Nadine. She is known as the Queen of purple and clean. When you get to her door you will see no one likes purple more. She has purple gifts here, there, and every where. She likes to give them away to children who like to take a bath everyday.

She gives away fun to little ones who do not run away when it is that time of day. She makes it so fun to take a bath at night, it just does not seem right to turn out the light without a special clean rub in the magical purple tub. It is coming to the end of the day and she will help you sleep, dream, and not peep, about Purples and Murples in a special way.

Now it is morning and we see Patti with her special Hattie. She will start to cook and you will eat and take a look. We will walk and talk with a special lady who will keep us well and swell. Her name is Sharon, and her game is to make us healthy which really makes us wealthy.

If you follow her lead and get plenty of exercise, food and fresh air, you will plant a health seed, for your family so near and dear, that we all need. As you walk along and talk to her, she will make you giggle and smile for sure. If you or someone does not feel well today, she will teach you how to try and make it go away.

As we start to walk back to the rain station, we will walk down a special trail to other special relations.

You will be introduced to a special Murple named J.K. and she is really swell and a friend of Okay.
She is in charge of imagination, for tomorrow and for this day. She will teach you in her own way,
to dream while you are young and dream when you are old, or so the story is told. I know people that
meet her are sold, and never seem to get old, because of her special way they never want to go away.

She will continue with you down the trail, walking as slow as a snail, as she wants you to dream and imagine along the way, and come back and tell her what you have dreamed, on another day.

When you walk down the trail as slow as a snail, you will get to meet and greet Steve I, he is such a kind guy. He is the keeper of animals here and he holds them so dear. He teaches us all about what they have to say each and every-day, and how they go about their lives and on their way.

He tells us how we need to protect them and nurture, to make sure they have a safe future. Without a blink he gets us to think, about taking care of them in a special way throughout all the days.

When you continue down the trail, you will meet a nice fellow, and yes he is dressed in yellow. He is very tall and his name is Paul. The story has it he use to play basketball. It may seem at odds, but he talks to all the Gods.

He says they all get along and so should we. They give us so many beautiful places.
We should love all their faces, understand, embrace, and hug all the different graces.
Now we find that we really are all together no matter what the weather.

Now we walk to a special building where they make Purple and words, and Murples run the machine that teach us nouns and verbs. They take the wheel barrow of letters and in the top they pour, and out comes the words, Purple, and more. We will learn more about this on our next trip for sure.

Our first trip to Purpleumpkin is almost over. We know when people come and stay they do not want to go away. When you come back soon in your own way, you can teach us what you have learned to say. Please, Thankyou, and Okay can hardly wait for that day. Come love, and travel again with us to a special place, where people have a special grace, and the sky is as soft as purple lace.

DRAW & DREAM HERE

DRAW & DREAM HERE

DRAW & DREAM HERE

DRAW
& DREAM HERE